NOËL

FOR JEANNE-MARIE

BY

Françoise

Charles Scribner's Sons New York

FIRST EDITION

It is winter time.
The snow is falling.
Jeanne-Marie
says to
her white sheep
Patapon:
"Noël will soon be here.
I am so happy,
so happy, Patapon."

Patapon answers:
"Noël?
I do not know about Noël.
Tell me about Noël,
Jeanne-Marie?
Tell me about Noël."
"Listen, Patapon,"
says Jeanne-Marie.
"Noël is the birthday of
the little Jesus."

"And there is something
more about Noël.
If you are very good,
Father Noël brings you
presents.
He comes in the night.
No one sees him,
no one at all.
I put my wooden shoes
near the chimney
and Father Noël fills them
with presents.
You will see, Patapon,
you will see...."

Patapon jumps
in the gold brown hay.
Patapon answers:
"I have four little black shoes.
But I can't take them off
and I can't put them
near the chimney.
Father Noël
will not leave any present
for me,
Jeanne-Marie."

"Patapon,"
says Jeanne-Marie,
"what do you think
Father Noël
will bring to me?
Maybe a bright red kerchief
with little white stars,
Patapon."

Patapon answers:
"Yes, you will
get a new bright red
kerchief.
But I have no shoe
to put near the chimney,
and Father Noël
won't leave
any present for me,
Jeanne-Marie."

"Patapon,"
says Jeanne-Marie,
"maybe Father Noël will
bring me
a new doll carriage.
And you, Patapon, you
will be the doll!
We'll have
lots and lots of fun,
riding in the country!"

Patapon answers:
"Yes–but I have no shoe
and Father Noël will not leave
any present for me."

"Patapon," says Jeanne-Marie
"Maybe I'll get a manger,
with the 'santons'–
the little Jesus,
the ox and the ass, the Kings,
and all the little people
who come to see the baby
and to bring him gifts."

Patapon answers:
"Yes, you will get a manger,
with all the little people:
the shepherds and the sheep,
and the Kings
with their gifts.
But I have no shoe
to put near the chimney,
and Father Noël
will not leave any present
for me,
Jeanne-Marie!"

"Patapon,"
says Jeanne-Marie,
"if you are very good
maybe you will get something,
anyway."
So Jeanne-Marie
goes to the old man
who makes wooden shoes.
She buys a tiny pair
for Patapon.

Now it is the night
before Christmas.
Jeanne-Marie puts her
best wooden shoes
near the chimney.
She puts Patapon's little
new ones near by.
Then Jeanne-Marie
goes to sleep.
And listen!
Do you
know what happened?

Father Noël
came in the night.

No one saw him.
No one at all.
Not even lambs.
Not even Patapon,
for Patapon
was fast asleep
in the gold brown hay.
But...

On Christmas morning
all the little santons
were smiling
in Jeanne-Marie's shoes.

And . . . and . . . in the tiny
wooden shoes
there was a present
for Patapon, too–
a yellow satin ribbon
with a bow,
and a tinkling bell!

Patapon was so pleased
with her present
that she jumped here and there
in the gold brown hay,
Ding! Ding! Ding! sang the
little bell.
Noël! Noël! Noël!